SIGMUND BROUWER

SHOCK WAVE

orca soundings

ORCA BOOK PUBLISHERS

Published in Canada and the United States in 2024 by Orca Book Publishers.
orcabook.com

Library and Archives Canada Cataloguing in Publication
Title: Shock wave / Sigmund Brouwer.
Names: Brouwer, Sigmund, 1959- author.
Series: Orca soundings.
Description: Series statement: Orca soundings
Identifiers: Canadiana (print) 20230558666 | Canadiana (ebook) 20230558674 |
ISBN 9781459839625 (softcover) | ISBN 9781459813816 (PDF) |
ISBN 9781459813946 (EPUB)
Subjects: LCGFT: Novels.
Classification: LCC PS8553.R68467 S55 2024 | DDC jC813/.54—dc23

Library of Congress Control Number: 2023947967

Summary: In this high-interest accessible novel for teen readers,
eighteen-year-old Jake is targeted by a crime boss after he
unwittingly helps a teen girl break into a houseboat.

Orca Book Publishers is committed to reducing the consumption
of nonrenewable resources in the production of our books. We make
every effort to use materials that support a sustainable future.

Orca Book Publishers gratefully acknowledges the support for its publishing
programs provided by the following agencies: the Government of Canada,
the Canada Council for the Arts and the Province of British Columbia
through the BC Arts Council and the Book Publishing Tax Credit.

Design by Ella Collier
Edited by Gabrielle Prendergast
Cover photography by Jess Craven/Stocksy.com

Printed and bound in Canada.

27 26 25 24 • 1 2 3 4

This book is dedicated

to the real Angela Wintar.

Chapter One

"Hey," the girl said. "Military brat like you want to take me on a boat ride after midnight, help assassinate someone?"

Jake sat in a lawn chair at the end of the dock behind his uncle's cottage, enjoying the sun and the view of the steep hills on the other side of the water. The girl had just arrived on a Jet Ski, tied it to a post, then stepped onto the dock, dripping lake water off her long, tanned legs. She was about his age, maybe a little older.

Her hands were on her hips as she waited for his response, like she was trying to put on a good show.

Jake had to admit the show was better than good. She wore a black bikini, and she had a beautiful face framed by long red hair and expensive sunglasses.

Jake fought two impulses. The first was to give in to his wiring and immediately agree to help, no matter what she asked. He wouldn't apologize for that impulse. The power of attraction was one of the main reasons the human race continued to exist.

His second impulse was stubborn refusal. Growing up in the military with a mom who went into battle carrying a stretcher, you learned there were things that mattered infinitely more than what you looked like. It was more important who you were under artillery fire, as you scrambled to reach injured soldiers who would bleed out unless you got them to medics in time. A girl in a bikini thinking she owned the world because she was pretty wasn't going to measure up.

He realized both impulses were shallow judgments based solely on her appearance. He shouldn't roll over for her just because she looked great. Nor should he assume that because she looked great she thought she owned the world.

Maybe, he thought wryly, actually talking to her might be the smart thing to do.

"My name is Jake Ballard," he said as she took the chair beside him. She lifted her sunglasses and hit him full voltage with eyes that were uncanny blue. "Nice to meet you."

"Angela Wintar," she said. She put the sunglasses back in place.

"Didn't know I had military tattooed all over me," he said.

"Sicamous is a small town. This is your uncle's place. He likes to take *Shock Wave*, tie up at the pier on the channel and have lunch at the restaurant that overlooks the water."

Shock Wave. That was the name of his uncle's boat. Twin electric motors. Fast. Quiet.

"Heard your mom is in the military," she continued. "Guessed you were a typical military brat. You move around a lot as a kid?"

"Yeah," Jake said.

He didn't offer more.

She gave a small shrug, like she was okay with his silence.

"Not curious about the assassination?" she asked.

His turn for a small shrug. He assumed it was some kind of game. Death—even in game form—wasn't something Jake considered trivial. Not with what he knew his mom had faced far too often during her time as a medical tech for the armed forces. And not with her mental-health struggles a year and half after retirement.

"It's this thing," she said. "With our friend group. We party on houseboats."

Sicamous. On a narrow channel with Mara Lake on one side and Shuswap Lake on the other side. Called itself the houseboat capital. Literally hundreds to rent and take out on the seemingly endless lake with arms that reached into four different mountain valleys.

When he said nothing, she continued.

"I'd like to win," she said. "Take me tonight on the lake, on the electric boat. We'd be like ghosts. I could be in and out of the houseboat before any of them woke up. I 'assassinate' them with a lipstick mark on the forehead. Then you can party with us later, when we show the photo to prove we did it."

Jake's uncle wasn't here. The cottage was his vacation property. Jake had spent more than a few summers out here as a kid. His uncle had taught him how to use the boat. How to water-ski. He'd invited Jake here again while his mom visited Toronto, giving Jake time to figure out what he wanted to do next, after his graduation from high school a month earlier. It had seemed like a good idea. Instead all the alone time had allowed Jake to brood about his resentment of the military. How he was expected to follow in his father's footsteps. The same father who'd given his life for the military. How did *that* make sense?

"So," Angela said, lifting her sunglasses again. "In?"

Might be nice to have a distraction from the brooding, Jake thought. What she was offering was just a stupid game. Not like it could lead to any trouble.

"Sure," he said. "Why not."

Chapter Two

As a military brat, Jake Ballard couldn't think of a more perfect situation for an assassination.

It was three in the morning. Hands on the wheel, he stood behind the windshield of *Shock Wave*. Every cruising light off. Drifting on black, calm water. Air completely still. Only sound the buzzing of insects. A smell of pine trees.

"Bet you wish it was cloudy," Jake said to Angela. Low voice. A mountain lake, this time of night, this situation, called for a low voice.

To Jake's right, steep, high hills formed a black cutout against the starlit sky. To his left, the silver of the moon shimmered on tiny ripples left behind by the curved hull.

Ahead of Jake, near the shoreline where trees came down to the water's edge, was an anchored houseboat. No lights. Quiet.

He wasn't much farther offshore, but the green-yellow dials on the boat's depth finder showed three hundred feet. Where the houseboat was, maybe thirty feet. Otherwise the anchor wouldn't hold. Easy to picture those hills dropping just as steeply beneath the surface as they rose into the sky.

Angela had been seated beside him the entire way, a white glow from her phone showing the features of her face as she concentrated on a GPS marker, pointing Jake in a straight line to a location about a half hour from his uncle's dock.

Then she'd turned off the phone and asked him to cut the power. It was a short swim from where they now drifted to the houseboat.

"We come all this way, just the two of us," Angela answered, equally low voice, "and those are the first words out of your mouth? That I wish it was cloudy?"

"For your assassination. Less likely anyone on the houseboat sees you."

"People rent houseboats to party. It's three in the morning. Lights off. Probably would take a cannon to wake them up at this point."

Angela stood. She slipped out of a pair of sweatpants. She pulled the bottom of her T-shirt up and over her head and dropped it at her bare feet. It revealed the same black bikini she'd worn that afternoon on his uncle's dock. Her shoulders, belly and legs were pale in the moonlight.

Angela moved to the back of the ski boat, where

a swim ladder reached into the water. She put one leg over, ready to climb down.

"Snorkel bag?" she said, voice still low.

She'd taken it on board and left it at the center of the boat. It was like a black fanny pack, but with glossy waterproof material on the exterior.

Jake picked it up. He felt three small tubes inside the otherwise flat pouch. One, he guessed, was her bright red lipstick. To paint a bullet hole on her victim's forehead. The other, maybe a flashlight. The third tube? He had no guesses.

The boat swayed slightly as he moved to the back. He handed her the bag.

She zipped it open, dropped her phone inside, zipped it shut. Strapped it around her waist, snapped the buckle shut.

She slid into the water.

"I won't be long," she said.

She began to swim through that black, calm water. No lights. Quiet.

People rent houseboats to party. It's three in the morning. Lights off. Probably would take a cannon to wake them up at this point.

Maybe Angela really was here to win a game. But Jake also realized that people on vacation took all their valuables onto the houseboat, as they would if they'd stayed in a hotel room. Valuables that could fit into a waterproof snorkel bag. Like cash and credit cards taken from wallets and purses. Like jewelry.

This could just as easily be a brilliant break and enter, with Jake the unwitting helper.

That meant the smartest thing Jake could do for himself was power up the twin electric outboard motors of his uncle's boat and head back down the lake.

If she was telling the truth about an assassination game, he'd be leaving her behind with friends. She could paint her friend's forehead with lipstick, take the photo, wake everyone up and claim victory.

If it wasn't a game, and they were caught in an act of burglary, it would be difficult to explain to a judge that he'd been innocent. Worse, he'd disappoint his mom.

It was just as unthinkable to help Angela if she returned to the boat with stolen property and wanted a successful escape. Jake was not a thief. Nor would he assist her in theft.

Yes, leaving as silently as he had arrived would be the smart move.

It wasn't like she might drown once she discovered he was gone. Not with such a short swim—either back to the houseboat or to shore. If she swam to shore, she'd be okay. It was a warm summer night. Worst thing she'd face were mosquitos. She could wait till dawn and look for a passing boater to pick her up.

Jake made his decision.

Chapter Three

He stayed. Drifting in the dark. Because if she was on the houseboat to rob someone, leaving her behind to swim to shore with stolen property wouldn't change the fact that he'd been part of it.

Each minute passed with Jake watching for houseboat lights to see if she'd get caught—either as a pretend assassin or a burglar.

A streak in the sky drew his attention. It traced a straight downward line, then faded. Meteor. Probably only the size of a pebble as it hit the atmosphere at thousands of miles per hour, burning up from friction against air. Glowing bright in destruction, as if defying its fate. A brief existence on earth.

Yeah. Brief life on earth. Dust to dust and all that.

Jake wasn't surprised that even a shooting star made him think about death. It had been on his mind a lot, especially this week. His mom was in Toronto, taking a course that might help her with PTSD and depression. Not easy for her, living with memories of picking up stretchers that weighed so little you knew you were carrying a child who had been at the wrong place and wrong time when bombs hit. Jake had been arguing a lot with her about why she'd stayed in the military after his dad died. He knew his anger about it wasn't helping her.

He'd call her when he had a chance, see how it went and do his best not to let his resentment show at the reason she was in Toronto.

He heard a slight splash. A fish jumping?

As Jake waited, he glanced at the stars, trying to enjoy the dusting of light against the sky, the buzzing of insects, on an evening so still the lake was like black porcelain. It only made him think about the military again. Would have been nice to have evenings like this with a father.

The houseboat remained shrouded in darkness.

His only warning of Angela's return was the sound of water dripping onto water as she rose up the ladder.

Jake didn't say anything obvious like *Hey, you're back.*

Instead he grabbed a towel, handing it to her in silence.

"Thanks," she said.

"You bet," Jake said.

He gave her time to towel off. She unsnapped the snorkel bag, set it on a seat. From his position, he couldn't determine if the snorkel bag had anything else in it. Like cash or jewelry.

Angela found her T-shirt, put it on again. Then her sweatpants.

She pulled her phone out of the snorkel bag. It brightened as she touched the screen.

"Ready with GPS," she said.

"Assassination a success?"

"That's why I'm ready with GPS," she answered. "Let's go."

Jake made no move to start the outboard. "Mind showing me the photo?"

"Photo?"

"Lipstick on the forehead," he said. "Giving you the victory assassination."

"You don't believe me?"

"Just want to share the victory."

"You don't believe me."

"And while you're at it, mind handing me the snorkel bag? And give me permission to go through it?"

"You're kidding me," she said.

"Nope."

"You're thinking you'll find what?"

"What I don't want to find is anything from a houseboat that belongs to someone else."

She didn't respond for several seconds, as if absorbing the words and what it meant.

"Wow," she said finally. Flat tone. "You got me. I ripped them off. Want to share half?"

"Nope. We'll just return it. All of it."

"Again, you're serious?"

"What I'm serious about is this. I'd like to see your victory photo. And an empty snorkel bag. Otherwise we make a short trip over to the houseboat and I wake everyone up."

"You're bringing down the mood. You know that, right?"

"This boat has a nice loud horn," he said. "You've got ten seconds."

"Again, wow. Didn't know I was on a ride with the morality police."

"Eight."

She sighed and flipped him the snorkel bag.

The pouch felt flatter, but that could have been his imagination. It held the same three small tubes. Lipstick. And probably flashlight. He zipped it open. Yes. Lipstick. Flashlight. He held it and clicked it on. It had a tiny pencil beam that showed the other tube in the snorkel bag. Pepper spray.

"Wow," Jake said, in a tone mocking the way she'd said it. "Pepper spray. This assassination game must be dangerous."

When she ignored the comment, Jake zipped the flashlight back into the pouch. "How about showing me the photo?"

"Really?"

"Really."

The phone screen brightened again. She turned it toward him. He stepped closer.

There it was. A photo of someone, from the neck up, asleep on a striped pillow. Dyed blond crew cut.

Wide face. Nose looked like it had been broken, like maybe in football as a linebacker. Eyes closed. The center of his forehead showed a bright-red bull's-eye, drawn with lipstick.

"Happy?"

"Yup," Jake said. Although he wasn't. He'd essentially accused her of being a thief. Wrongly accused her.

"I'm not," she said. "Take me back."

She didn't speak another word, not even goodbye as she walked away from his uncle's dock, leaving him alone to tie the ski boat in place, knowing he totally deserved her anger.

As distractions went, not so good.

Chapter Four

Jake heard the rumble of approaching Harley motor-
cycles from the road behind his uncle's cottage.

It was closing in on noon. Jake sat in one of the
pair of chairs his uncle had arranged at the end of
the dock. Tied to the dock beside him was *Shock
Wave*. He was on his third cup of coffee, enjoying the
warmth of the sun.

To Jake's right was the full extent of Mara Lake,
with rising hills on each side. Technically Mara Lake
was a widening of the Shuswap River, which

emptied through the Sicamous Narrows into the larger Shuswap Lake on the other side.

The resort town of Sicamous bordered the east side of the narrows. This short passage took boaters past the commercial docks of Sicamous. Condo buildings. Bars and restaurants. All part of a town with a permanent population of about 2,500. Summertime, of course, it had a lot more people than that.

When the rumble of the Harleys shut down, Jake cocked his head. He'd expected the bikers to continue on down the road.

He wondered if the now silent Harleys were on the driveway of his uncle's summer cottage.

Jake stood and took a couple of strides down the dock, toward the house.

He stopped midstep as a visitor rounded the corner of the house and approached the dock. He was bald, round-faced and overweight, wearing a Hawaiian shirt and shorts and flip-flops. His face was sunburned red.

The guy carried what looked like a short-nosed pistol. Jake felt his heart jump into high gear.

"Hey," the guy said, now only a couple of steps away. "Nice day, am I right? Hope you don't mind. I parked my car out front with some friends."

The cheerfulness was strange, considering the weapon in the man's hand. The guy pointed the pistol at him.

"Jake Ballard," Hawaiian Shirt said, "I'm guessing you know what I'm holding here. Military background and all."

Jake knew. The end of the pistol was not a black hole. It was covered with a bright-yellow cap. If the man in the Hawaiian shirt pulled the trigger, it would fire two darts, connected by wire to the pistol. The darts would embed in Jake and deliver enough electrical voltage to paralyze him.

A Taser pistol. Aimed at Jake.

Huh, Jake thought. The guy knew not only who Jake was but also enough about him to know that he would recognize the weapon. Jake felt more than a tremble of nervousness. Which made him angry. Which made him determined not to let the guy see a trace of his fear.

Hawaiian Shirt tossed the Taser at Jake, who caught it in two hands. Then the man eased himself into one of the deck chairs. "Your uncle has a nice place."

Jake handed him back the Taser gun. "I'm guessing you don't have a permit for this."

That helped him past his nerves, letting him find a way to remain casual.

"Well, this will be interesting," Hawaiian Shirt said.

Jake said nothing. Sat back in the chair. Grabbed his coffee.

"I show up with a Taser so that you know I mean business," Hawaiian Shirt said. "I give it to you so that you'll be in control and relaxed enough to answer my questions. And you give it right back. Why?"

Jake sipped on his coffee, trying to figure out the guy's angle.

"Come on, kid," Hawaiian Shirt said. "I already like how you handle yourself. Humor me, okay? Why give it back?"

"If you really wanted to hurt me, you never would have given it to me in the first place."

"Good call. I don't want to hurt you. I just want my money back. And my Daytona."

"Money? Daytona?"

"My watch. Rolex. Watch like that, you want everyone to see it. I wear it all day. Nighttime, though, I wear a Fitbit to track sleep. Still have the Fitbit. But the Daytona, not so much. Give it back, along with the money, and we'll be good."

"I don't have anything of yours," Jake said.

Hawaiian Shirt sighed. He dug into the right front pocket of his shorts and pulled out a phone. First a brief pause for facial recognition to unlock it.

Then he pushed the screen with his forefinger and put the phone on speaker.

Jake heard the phone ring.

A male voice answered, "Standing by."

"I like the kid. How about move into place, and I'll do my best to keep this friendly." Hawaiian Shirt hung up and spoke to Jake. "One of the reasons I took my time getting here was that I was waiting for some friends from a gang in Kamloops. The ones I followed in my car to the driveway out front."

Jake turned his head to look.

Three of them rounded the corner of the cottage. Men. Midtwenties. All very large. Wearing sunglasses and leather vests covered with patches. They had massive arms, dark with tattoos.

A gang in Kamloops. As in motorcycle gang. They walked across the lawn toward the lake, stepped onto the dock and stopped. They crossed those massive arms across their chests and waited.

Chapter Five

"Jake William Ballard," Hawaiian Shirt said to Jake. "Eighteen years old. Both parents military. First three years of your life you lived at an Armed Forces base in Kingston. Then another two years at CFB Moose Jaw. Followed by CFB North Bay, Shilo and, most recently, CFB Suffield. Your father was killed in action just as you turned four. Your mother is Master Corporal Leona Ballard, retired a year ago as a medical technician for the army. After your father's death, she did tours in Afghanistan, Libya and Kuwait. Your uncle Mike Ballard, your dad's brother, currently in Calgary at his stockbroker company, owns this vacation property as well as a luxury condo in Calgary, both mortgage-free, and two Ferraris. Plus a Beemer parked here. Of most importance to this conversation, his fire insurance will fully cover any and all damages to this property and his Calgary condo and his cars. Wish I could promise to burn down your mom's place instead, but the two of you have been renting your entire lives. Nothing you own that you'll hate to lose. His stuff is the only leverage I have. If you go to your mom or the cops with any of this, I promise, everything your uncle owns will be ashes."

Jake's heart rate continued to rise. This guy had just threatened him with arson?

"At this point," Hawaiian Shirt continued, "most people would ask how I know all this. Yet you don't. I like your style, I really do, this whole watchful-panther-waiting-to-strike vibe you have. Because I like you, if you give me back the Daytona and the money, we're even. My guys don't lay a finger on you. Nothing goes wrong with your uncle's nice properties or vehicles."

Jake said, "I don't know who you are or why you're here."

Hawaiian Shirt gave a nod at the ski boat. "How many boats with that name?"

Shock Wave. Painted in bold, flowing letters.

"There's a bar along the Sicamous Narrows with a security camera," Hawaiian Shirt said. "Video footage shows you in the ski boat, passing the camera at around 2:30 a.m., outbound to the Shuswap. *Shock Wave* shows up bright and clear. Then again, same boat, inbound to Mara Lake at around 4:00 a.m. Looks like you had a passenger, but footage doesn't show who."

Hawaiian Shirt continued in a friendly tone. "I like knowing how things work. Heard of AirTags, tracking devices about the size of a quarter? An AirTag sends out a Bluetooth signal. Drop it in a forest, nobody knows where it is. What's needed is a nearby device on Apple's network to detect the signal and send it to iCloud. Not a bad system, considering the many millions, maybe billions, of devices in the world. Once the AirTag connects to a nearby device, then the person who owns it can find it on a map. You're with me so far, right?"

Jake nodded.

"Let me tell you about a specific AirTag that went missing during the night," Hawaiian Shirt said. "I wait and wait and sure enough, about three hours ago, someone with a device gets near enough to pick up the signal. Is that about when you came here on the dock with a phone in your pocket? Your phone triggering the AirTag? Three hours is plenty of time for all my research and to call in a favor from a club in Kamloops. Before we met, what I wanted to decide was whether you knew the money would be on my houseboat and if somebody sent you from Vancouver. That's not on my radar anymore. Good thing. Otherwise this would have been complicated and messy. Would have involved body parts. Yours and theirs. Instead I just want my property back."

"I don't have anything that belongs to you."

Hawaiian Shirt pulled out his phone again. "No? Something else about AirTags, in case you didn't know. This Find My app is slick. Get near your AirTag, and you can play a sound."

He squinted as he scrolled on the screen.

A high-pitched beeping came from the cushions at the back of the ski boat. After a few seconds it faded.

"Almost like magic," said Hawaiian Shirt. "That's the AirTag inside my wallet. The one you stole from me last night from a houseboat. Along with my Daytona. Did you even know that model of Rolex is worth seventy grand? Or was that as random as finding the missing bundles of hundred-dollar bills that I'll want back along with my wallet and my watch?"

Chapter Six

Final words from Hawaiian Shirt on the dock. *I don't care if it was a girl named Angela or Godzilla himself who took the money. I just want it back. Along with my Daytona. So if she really is the thief, it's on you to track her down. You've got till 10:00 a.m. tomorrow morning. Otherwise expect fire trucks. Lots of them.*

Four hours had passed since the warning. Jake stood in the doorway of a small office, sunglasses on the top of his head, as the manager of Houseboats

Vay-Cay responded to the question Jake had just asked.

"Nobody named Angela works here, and if even she did, she was wrong about job openings. We've got nothing right now. Try back in a couple of weeks. You never know." She was midforties, black shirt, black jeans. Deep tan. Sun-streaked hair. She didn't get out from behind her desk. Just kept her hands on the keyboard.

As job applications went, this was a quick rejection. Jake hadn't even managed to sit down in the chair opposite the manager's desk. Behind her the wall was lined with large photos of houseboats in different beautiful lake settings.

"In a couple weeks, sure," Jake said, giving a slight nod. "Hope you don't mind a quick question."

"As long as it's quick. This is our craziest time of year."

"All these rental houseboats. You've got GPS locators on them, right?"

"You know how much those things are worth? How little experience most people have when they rent them? How much booze they drink? Nighttime, they're not allowed to run the boat. It moves, it sets off alarms for us. Simple rule. Anchor near shore after dark. I could pull up a map of the Shuswap and show you the exact location of each one of them right now. But I won't. Too much stuff to do. If you get the hint."

"Got it." Jake flipped on his sunglasses. "And thanks."

He stepped back outside into bright sunshine. It was 3:00 p.m. now. Clock ticking.

Seagulls circled overhead, their squawking breaking up the sound of an approaching motor-boat. The surface of Mara Lake glistened blue in a long ribbon to the horizon of the far hills. All the houseboat rentals started on Mara Lake. From here they cruised through the Sicamous Narrows past the town on the right side, under a highway bridge and into the much, much larger Shuswap, with hundreds of miles of shoreline.

Yet Angela had taken them straight to the houseboat the night before. Because she knew exactly where to find it thanks to its GPS locator.

Jake walked away from the office—a small industrial trailer baking in the sunlight—toward the bike rack. He could have borrowed his uncle's BMW, but job searching in an $80,000 car didn't look good. Not that he wanted this job. He'd just wanted to find out if Angela worked for a houseboat company.

People rent houseboats to party. It's three in the morning. Lights off. Probably would take a cannon to wake them up at this point.

All he knew was that Angela had targeted someone who'd rented a houseboat. If she knew that houseboat's GPS location, she must have some kind of connection to one of the houseboat rental companies. Learning about the GPS locators had just strengthened Jake's assumption.

Because it had been so dark the night before, Jake had seen no markings on the houseboat to identify the rental company that owned it. That meant going from company to company on a mountain bike. He'd already visited six. And all six used GPS to locate their houseboats.

Just before he reached his bike, his phone buzzed. He recognized the number.

Jake pulled his earbuds from his front pocket, popped them in place and accepted the call.

"Antoine," Jake said.

Corporal Antoine DePruis. Jake could picture him easily. Cropped hair with lots of gray. Short. Muscular. Intense. Fast-moving. Fast-talking with a Quebecois accent in his English. He'd begun as a combat soldier, moved up the ranks and out of the field and was now stationed at CFB Petawawa, north of Toronto.

"A couple of things," Antoine said. "With no apologies that it's taken so long to get back to you. I had to call a friend who had to call a friend. You know how connected we are in the military family. Not sure if you're going to like the answer."

Chapter Seven

"What's the answer I'm not going to like?" Jake asked, seagulls still circling above.

"So much like your dad. He always wanted to get straight to the point."

Almost fifteen years had passed since Antoine had helped place a Canadian flag across the coffin of Sergeant William Ballard, but Antoine still found a way to bring every conversation back to Jake's father. Jake couldn't remember him leaving for Afghanistan or his body being returned.

He had no memories at all of his father. Just a legacy of newspaper articles, his mother's stories and a medal of honor. Bitter consolation for what had been taken from Jake by an enemy's sniper bullet on a cold winter day halfway across the world.

"We all miss him," Jake said. Because it was expected.

"So I didn't do this favor for you. I'm doing it for him. Got it?"

"Ten-four." Jake knew Antoine liked it when he used military terms. "Any luck with the name?"

Jake wheeled his bike out of the rack, thinking about the final words from Hawaiian Shirt. *You've got till 10:00 a.m. tomorrow morning. Otherwise expect fire trucks. Lots of them.*

He didn't want to waste time staying in one spot to finish the conversation. He slipped the phone back into his pocket. With his earbuds, he was hands-free.

As Jake waited for Antoine to answer, he jumped on the bike and began to pedal. Maybe ten minutes down the road to the next place. Sun Daze Houseboats.

"Happy to let you know my connections came through and I found a military cop to to run the name for me," Antoine said. "Nothing on any database shows the existence of an Angela Wintar, approximate age eighteen to twenty-two. Not in British Columbia, not anywhere in Canada. The only Angela Wintar she could find is a retired principal from a Catholic school in the Hamilton area. So I doubt she's the one you want. But I looked up this Angela Wintar on Facebook to be sure. She's out in the Maritimes now. Runs an Airbnb place."

Not much of a surprise to Jake. She'd been smart enough to figure out how to burglarize a houseboat. Not likely she'd have used her real name with Jake.

Jake had other questions too. How had she known to target someone with a $70,000 Rolex?

Where had she hidden the watch and bundle of money before getting onto the ski boat?

"Still doing the martial-arts thing?" Antoine asked.

Moving every few years meant that military brats always had to prove themselves as the new kid in a new school. And military brats tended not to have the most fashionable clothing, which set them apart even more. Early on Jake had decided it was easier to fight a bully than ignore a bully. Didn't always work with keeping teachers or principals or his mom happy, but it sure worked against bullies.

"Each new base," Jake said, "there's always some combat specialist who likes teaching me new moves."

There was a pause, like Antoine had been asking about martial arts to avoid asking a difficult question but was now finally going to ask.

"Why do you want me to keep this from your mom? And the local police? If you're in some kind of drug trouble—"

"You know me better than that."

"And you're not stalking this Angela."

Jake heard his voice get sharp. "To repeat, you know me better than that."

"I don't like keeping secrets from your mom."

If you go to your mom or the cops with any of this, I promise, everything your uncle owns will be ashes.

"You'll have to trust me on this," Jake said. "How about I explain later?"

There was a pause, then Antoine said, "All you wanted me to do was reach out to someone in the military police to run a name. Done. No results. Anything else?"

"Thanks. I owe you. Got to run."

You've got till 10:00 a.m. tomorrow morning. Otherwise, expect fire trucks. Lots of them.

Chapter Eight

"Hi," Jake said. "I met a girl in town last night. Maybe a little older than me. Long red hair. She said I should stop by here to look for work."

That was how he'd started his conversations already at the other houseboat companies.

"Red hair?" The guy in front of Jake grinned, showing perfect teeth. He was Asian, probably late twenties. Dark round sunglasses. Wearing shorts and a Sun Daze Houseboats T-shirt, both arms heavily tattooed. He had a walkie-talkie clipped to his belt. "Don't need to say more than that. If Ashley sent you here to look for work, expect to start tomorrow."

Ashley.

Jake felt like he'd just pulled a slot handle and a bunch of coins were tumbling out in front of him.

"How'd you like the place?"

"Place?" Jake said.

"The Crow's Nest," Round Sunglasses said. "She wouldn't have been any other place. Bartends there just about every night. Guess Nepto must have been at the gym. Otherwise she would have introduced you to him."

"Nepto?"

"Blaine Nepto. The manager. You'll find him in one of three places. Here. The gym. Or the Crow's Nest. If she said you should talk to him about a job, you've got a job. Whatever she wants, Nepto gives her. Just don't tell him I said that."

Round Sunglasses gave a sly smile. "Not that I blame him. Come on, you met her. And don't tell him I said that either."

"Not a chance," Jake said. He wasn't sure he even needed to talk to Nepto. He'd learned what he wanted to know. The name of the bar where she worked. Her first name. From here he could easily track her down, even if it meant another call to Antoine.

"Just head there." Round Sunglasses pointed at a houseboat docked at the end of the wharf. "He's checking it out for a damage-deposit return."

Before Jake could respond, Round Sunglasses unclipped his walkie-talkie and buzzed.

"Yeah," came the reply from the walkie-talkie.

"Got someone headed your way. Looking for a job."

"Not hiring," the voice said.

"Ashley sent him," Round Sunglasses said.

A pause. Then: "Send him."

At this point Jake couldn't turn back toward his mountain bike. He needed to keep the pretense going or Round Sunglasses would be puzzled. Maybe even mention it to Nepto, who might mention it to his girlfriend.

Besides, Jake didn't see that it would do any harm to see if he could learn anything more from Nepto.

Round Sunglasses clipped the walkie-talkie back in place and spoke to Jake. "Remember, what I said about her is between you and me. He's the jealous type. Nobody likes to be around when he loses it."

Jake gave Round Sunglasses a thumbs-up and headed toward the moored houseboat. While it was great that the guy had been so chatty, Jake didn't understand people like that, spilling whatever was on their minds. Maybe it was from a lifetime of going from base to base, moving so often that it didn't seem worthwhile to make friends. You got into the habit of staying self-contained. Watching instead of reaching out, getting involved.

As Jack stepped onto the dock—houseboats moored on both sides—he felt the buzz of an incoming text.

He glanced down at his phone as he walked.

You anywhere near the cottage?

It was a text from his uncle Mike.

Both hands on his phone, Jake used his thumbs to reply.

Easy biking distance. Maybe 20 minutes.

Three dots appeared on the screen, showing Mike was about to reply. Jake lifted his sunglasses to see better and left them on top of his head.

He glanced up to make sure he wasn't going to walk off the dock. Then another buzz, and he dropped his glance down to the phone again.

See if you can make it in 15. There's been a break-in. I'm on the phone right now with the security company, will call you as soon as I finish.

Security company? Break-in?

"Heads up, dude." The voice that broke into Jake's thoughts sounded irritated. "You the one looking for a job?"

Jake raised his head just in time to stop a collision. He'd been so focused on the texts, he didn't realize he'd almost reached the end of the dock.

The first thing that registered for Jake was doubt that the collision would have hurt the guy. He was body-builder big, body-builder wide, his Sun Daze Houseboats T-shirt stretched tight across his chest.

As Jake lifted his head higher to make eye contact, something else registered with a shock of recognition. Something of more significance. The guy had a dyed-blond crew cut. Wide face. Nose looked like it had been broken, like maybe in football as a linebacker.

He'd seen that face. The night before. In a photo. With a red-lipstick target on his forehead.

No lipstick on his forehead now. Just the furrows of a frown.

"Hey, sorry," Jake said. He held up his phone. "My uncle just texted me. Emergency. Got to run."

That's what Jake did.

Turned around and ran. Just as the sound of sirens reached him from the other side of the lake.

Chapter Nine

To get back to his uncle's property, Jake needed to head north through town, take the highway onto the high bridge that crossed the Sicamous Narrows, and take the first road south again.

He was pedaling as hard as he could, hardly even aware of how his lungs were heaving for breath. That was because all the way through town, he could see thick black smoke rising above the buildings that blocked his view of his uncle's property on the opposite shoreline.

Break-in *and* a fire?

When he reached the highest point of the bridge, Jake looked to his left for a better view of the properties along the east side of the lake.

The smoke had turned into a thin, rising wisp. He didn't know if that was good or bad. Good because the fire had been extinguished? Or bad because it had burned out?

It took just five minutes along the lakeshore road to get to his uncle's place once he'd crossed the bridge, but it was agony, his lungs fighting for air and his legs weak with exhaustion. From a couple hundred yards away, he saw the bright red of a massive fire truck in the driveway of his uncle's cottage. Along with an RCMP vehicle. The light bar from the fire truck threw out strobes of red and blue. No firefighters or RCMP in sight.

He reached the mailbox that marked the property line, not waiting to come to a full stop before leaping off the bicycle and letting it drop to the grass, and ran toward the house.

The front door was open, security alarm blaring. Jake took a long-enough look at the front door to see that it had been kicked open. The deadbolt had splintered the doorframe.

But there was no smell of smoke. It wasn't until he reached the living room with its view of the lake that he saw the firefighters and RCMP. Three firefighters, one police officer, standing on the dock, blocking his view of the ski boat, gazing down at it. All three firefighters were in full gear. But there was no fire hose in sight.

In that moment Jake had no doubt that Hawaiian Shirt had returned and set the ski boat on fire as a warning. He wondered if the fiberglass of the boat's hull would have created the thick oily smoke. And because it had been burning on water, there had been nothing for the firefighters to extinguish.

He bolted out through the back door and to the dock.

One of the firefighters—tall and bearded—turned at the thumping of Jake's footsteps on the dock. He held up his hand to stop Jake. "This your place?"

Jake nodded, hands on his knees, unable to talk as he gasped for air.

"Here's the situation. Someone placed a barrel filled with oily rags in the center of the ski boat at the dock. Lit the rags on fire. No damage to the ski boat. But they kicked in the door. You have the security code? That sound is driving me crazy."

Jake nodded again. He straightened, walked back to the house as his breathing began to return and punched in the numbers on the keypad. Instant silence.

That's when a woman walked into the kitchen. She must have come through the front door. This woman had the same kind of trim runner's build as Jake's mom. She wore Nike shoes, jeans and a blue hoodie. She also looked to be the same age as his mom. She had light brown skin and short-cropped, curly black hair beneath a ball cap with an emblem patch on the front. Jake assumed from the ball cap that she was with the fire department, but he was blinking sweat and couldn't quite focus his vision.

"You're Jake Ballard?" she asked with a friendly smile.

Jake wiped sweat from his forehead. He let out a huge breath. "Yeah."

"I'm Macy Templeton. Looks like Corporal DePruis had some good instincts about this situation."

Corporal DePruis? As in Antoine?

She kept that friendly smile on her face as she pulled a small wallet from her back pocket, flipped it open and stepped toward Jake.

"How about the two of us go. have a chat with the firefighters and RCMP?" she said. "Then we can jump in my car and find a restaurant that serves breakfast. No matter what time of day, I always think better after a good breakfast."

She handed him her identification.

She was closer now. Jake was tall enough to look directly ahead at the emblem on her ball cap. He wasn't blinking away sweat anymore and saw it more clearly. It was an emblem patch he recognized.

A glance at the identification in her wallet confirmed it for Jake.

Armed forces. Military police.

Chapter Ten

Macy Templeton's car was a black vintage Corvette, sleek and gleaming, right down to the chrome ball at the top of the stick shift. After a long chat with firefighters and police, she took Jake to the restaurant, running through the gears effortlessly, making his head snap back with the acceleration at every opportunity.

At the restaurant, they sat opposite each other in a booth by the window, where she had a good view of her parked Corvette. She had her laptop shut on the table. She ordered eggs over easy, sausage and pancakes, telling Jake that whatever he wanted to eat was on her.

He was thirsty because of the bike ride, so he was drinking lots of water. He wasn't that hungry and ate only half his burger, too worried about what Hawaiian Shirt might do next. Too aware that 10:00 a.m. the next morning was about sixteen hours away.

Macy didn't drop the small talk until after the waitress had taken away their plates and refilled her coffee.

"Now I can think," she said. "Let's start with this. Corporal DePruis knows something is up. He says you've never asked him for help with anything. Also says it's suspicious that you're hiding from him the fact that you are alone here and your mom is in Toronto."

She read the expression on Jake's face correctly. "Facebook. She's posted a few photos. He told me all this, and I'm thinking it's no big deal. But he insisted I look into this a bit beyond just running a name. Since I was on leave in Radium Hot Springs for some golf, I said I'd make a day trip here."

Jake knew Radium Hot Springs was a village in the mountains, almost at the Alberta border.

"On leave from…?"

"The base at Cold Lake. One of the few places you haven't been. So, given it's a nice day for a drive, I head out. Four-hour drive, took me less. Fun cruising through the mountains on a day like this. About twenty minutes out from here, I get a courtesy call from the Sicamous RCMP detachment. Security alarm at your uncle's place and—"

"RCMP?" Jake didn't want the RCMP involved. Next time, maybe, it would be the cottage on fire. Not just a pile of oily rags in a barrel.

"Right after talking to Antoine, I did the friend-of-a-friend thing. Military police often work with local law enforcement. We'll get help when needed.

First thing I did was call my friend, let him know I would be in the area, said I might need to ask for a favor. In return I promised to help them out if there was something they needed to know. And given what happened at your uncle's place, they have questions already. Any idea why someone went to all that work to get fire and police out there? All smoke, no fire?"

Jake didn't answer.

"My guess?" Macy said. "Somebody wanted to send you a message. Which means I have a couple of questions. Who? And why? I'm not here to judge. Drugs? You can tell me."

Jake met her gaze and didn't flinch. "Why are you here?"

"I told you. Corporal DePruis gave me a call."

"What I meant was, why drive four hours and take time from a golf vacation for this? You don't know him. You don't know me."

"I have to explain? Armed forces. We're family. He'd have my back if I needed him. And I've got yours.

I owe that to Antoine, and to your mom. I've seen her record. She's given a lot to the armed forces."

"Too much," Jake said.

"Meaning?"

Jake wasn't going to go there. Not with someone he didn't know. He ignored the question. "Yes. The fire was a message. I thought I could do this alone. If you're able to help, I'd like to handle this without anyone else finding out."

Macy said, "You need to tell me everything."

"Yesterday afternoon this girl, Ashley, showed up at my uncle's place. Told me her name was Angela."

Had it been only twenty-four hours since she had stepped onto his uncle's dock?

Jake gave Macy every detail as she sipped her coffee. Her eyes never left his face. When he finished, she stared out the window for a full minute before returning her gaze to him and asking a question.

"This guy with the Hawaiian Shirt. Why was he so sure it was you? Anyone could have thrown his wallet into the ski boat."

"He has video showing me, in my uncle's ski boat, passing by one of the bars along the water at two thirty in the morning."

"So many things to unpack," Macy said. "Which bar? How would he get that footage?"

"I wondered the same thing. But I figured the only thing within my control was to start looking for Angela—or Ashley, I guess. All of this depends on finding her."

Macy gave it more thought. Sipped her coffee again. "You're right. You have her first name, and you know where she works. That's a good start. We can take it from there."

"We?"

"We. You asked for my help. I'm on you like a tick on a hound. And I think we should bring your mom in on this."

"She's got enough to worry about. I'm asking for your help because I don't want this messing her up. When it's over, then I tell her."

"Deal," Macy said. "But if it looks like things are going sideways, I reserve the right to call in the RCMP at any time."

Jake didn't see much of a choice. And knowing he didn't have a choice gave him a sense of relief. Macy seemed competent, very competent.

He nodded.

Macy glanced at her watch. "Six o'clock. How about we visit the bar where Ashley works? I'm thinking you go in there alone. I'll wait out front, make a few calls. That should get us a list of renters from Sun Daze Houseboats, maybe the name of Hawaiian Shirt guy. I'll walk inside about ten minutes later to see how it's going. If she's not there, at least you'll have her last name and we can run it through the databases. Find out where she lives."

Jake nodded.

"Just to make sure you'll have my help anytime in there, if you need it, I want my number on your speed dial. Call the instant it looks like there is trouble. If you can't talk, I'll listen in."

Jake nodded again.

"Something to think about though," Macy said.

"Yes?"

"When you get the money back, then what? Really think a bundle of cash like that is clean? From a guy who hangs with bikers? And why is Hawaiian Shirt guy taking it out on a houseboat in the first place? I'm not recovering dirty money for anyone, and neither should you."

"I have an idea about that," Jake said. "But before I run it past you, are you able to check boat ownerships from your computer? I have another name for you. Blaine Nepto."

Chapter Eleven

The Crow's Nest bar was a couple of blocks in from the Sicamous Narrows, tucked between a grocery store and a drugstore. Because Jake had been coming to Sicamous every summer since he was a kid, he knew it was a less touristy bar. Out-of-towners wanted to be near the water, to watch boats cruise the channel.

It was in an old building with a faded brick exterior. The windows were small, with dark blinds, giving the place a dimly lit atmosphere even in the early evening when it was still bright outside.

Jake walked inside to loud conversation and even louder music. Stools lined the full length of the bar, and behind it neon signs glowed on the wall, advertising different brands of beer. All the tables were full. A busy evening at the Crow's Nest.

Jake wasn't legally old enough to order a drink with alcohol. That didn't matter, because he wasn't here for beer or cocktails.

He scanned the bar for a red-headed girl his age. The only bartender in sight was a middle-aged guy with a ponytail that would have barely looked good on someone twenty years younger.

Jake took a seat at the bar.

Ponytail pulled at a long handle to fill a few glasses with draft beer. He set them on the counter for a server, then moved to Jake.

"ID?" Ponytail asked.

"I'm here because I owe Ashley some money," Jake said. "I don't see her."

"She's not working tonight," Ponytail said. He used a rag to wipe the bar in front of Jake.

"When should I come back?" Jake asked.

"Nice try. We don't give out employee information. Especially about Ashley. You're in a long line of guys trying to find out more about her."

Jake hadn't expected this. And the clock was ticking.

"My advice?" Ponytail said, leaning forward. "Set your sights on someone else. Her boyfriend is here every evening. And he's right behind you."

Jake turned to look and almost hit a human wall.

Blaine Nepto was standing behind him, arms crossed, still in his Sun Daze Houseboats T-shirt. Two other guys of about the same age stood beside him, one on each side. One wore Ray-Ban sunglasses, even though it was dark inside the bar. The other had on an Edmonton Oilers ball cap. Both were shorter than Nepto, but all three, it was obvious, worked out.

"You asking about Ashley?" Nepto said. He grabbed Jake's right arm just above the elbow and pinched hard. "Let's go someplace less noisy."

"Nepto," Ponytail said. "Don't do anything that brings in cops again. You hear me?"

Jake allowed Nepto to guide him toward the back of the Crow's Nest. They moved past the bathrooms, then through a cluttered hallway to an emergency exit. Still gripping Jake's arm, Nepto pushed him outside.

A large dumpster in the alley shielded them from the view of passing traffic. The sunshine was bright. The air smelled like rotting bananas.

Nepto shoved Jake against the dumpster. He stepped back. Oilers Cap on one side. Ray-Ban on the other.

Jake was trapped.

"You're the guy who showed up looking for a job today. I talked to Ashley. She didn't send you. You saw my face and ran. Explain."

"What's to explain?" Jake said. "You know who I am. You needed my boat last night. Yours has electric outboards too. But it's in for repairs."

"He told you to explain about Ashley," Ray-Ban said as stepped forward and raised a fist. "Not his boat troubles."

"Anything but his face," Nepto said. "Don't mark him up. Remember what happened last time."

Just as he'd been taught countless times by some of the best combat fighters in the military, Jake noted the positions of his opponents. He mentally rehearsed the best sequence of events as if he were planning out dance moves.

He said to Ray-Ban, "Consider this a warning. Don't."

"Hit him," Nepto said.

It made it easier for Jake to know that Ray-Ban didn't want to mark up his face and would be going for a body punch. With his fist already at shoulder level, Ray-Ban was unlikely to swing downward. Instead he'd have to make a loop with his fist and come from below with an upper cut, aimed for Jake's gut. If it landed, Jake would be in trouble—Ray-Ban was a big man.

But big often meant slow. The punch seemed to come in a lazy arc, and Jake easily deflected it with his right forearm. In the same motion he kicked hard, planting the top of his foot squarely in Ray-Ban's crotch as if punting a football.

As Ray-Ban dropped to his knees in disbelief and agony, Jake was already spinning on one foot toward Oilers Cap. The obvious move was a side kick into the guy's kneecap, but that would put him in the hospital. Instead Jake sideslipped the incoming punch, moved in and landed a quick blow with two knuckles into the man's diaphragm. Oilers Cap dropped to his knees, gasping for air.

Jake stayed in motion, clearing the dumpster and putting a few steps between him and Nepto.

Now Nepto stood between Jake and the dumpster. He looked back and forth between Jake and his two friends on the ground. He seemed a little less sure of himself.

"Has Ashley left town yet?" Jake asked, ignoring the moans from Ray-Ban and Oilers Cap.

"How did you know she was leaving town?"

"Here's the important question," Jake said. "Is she leaving without you?"

"I'm driving her to Kelowna tonight," Nepto said. "She's flying out in the morning to visit her grandmother. She said she knew I wouldn't enjoy hanging around with a sick old person."

"At this point," Jake said, "what you need to ask yourself is how and why I guessed this. And the answer is, she is planning to leave with a bunch of money. Money she didn't tell you about."

"You're lying. Not Ashley."

"Either we talk to her or the cops will," Jake said. "You interested in cops finding out how you rob houseboats?"

Chapter Twelve

As Jake followed Nepto into the apartment building, he knew that Macy was tracking him with her Find My app on her phone. She'd have no trouble locating the address. But he didn't know if the app was precise enough to identify the apartment unit inside.

Jake pulled out his cell phone, made sure the volume was down and hit speed dial for Macy. Without ending the call, he slipped his cell phone into his back pocket, hoping Macy could hear him.

"You said apartment four, right?" Jake asked Nepto.

"Just stay with me," Nepto said. "And keep your mouth shut when we get there."

When they reached number four, Nepto unlocked and stepped inside. The apartment had an open layout, with a kitchen and dining room table off to one side.

"Ashley?"

She stepped out of the kitchen area into the living room. She was in jeans and a T-shirt, hair tied back.

There was a stack of mail on a side table. Jake glanced at the top envelope. Utility bill.

"Ashley Matteson," Jake said, reading the name on the envelope to pass along the information to Macy. "Nice to meet you under your real name."

"Shut up, smart guy," Nepto said.

"Nepto, what is going on?" Ashley said.

"He was looking for you at the Crow's Nest," Nepto said. "Somehow he knows a bunch of stuff. Way too much. Said unless he talked to you, he was going to the cops."

With Macy waiting out in front of the Crow's Nest, it had been a calculated risk to go with Nepto and leave her behind. But Jake had seen no other way to get to Ashley in time. Now, with Macy listening to the conversation, it felt less risky.

Ashley put a hand on her hip and stared at Jake the way she'd done on the dock the day before, in a bikini and pretending to be Angela Wintar.

"Nepto keeps an eye open for houseboat renters with something worth stealing," Jake said. "He has their GPS locations so you can find them easily at night. The two of you use his boat with nice, quiet electric outboards to rob them after they've partied too hard. Except his boat is in for repairs. So you used me and my boat."

"See?" Nepto said. "I told you we should have

just borrowed that outboard instead of getting him to take you out there."

"Rule one," Ashley said. "We don't take risks. Borrowing without permission is stealing. No good way of explaining it if caught. Unlike everything else that we can talk our way out of."

"Well, he figured it out," Nepto said. "And we're caught anyway. Now what?"

"We're totally clear," Ashley answered. "He was part of it. Means he is not going to go to the cops, because he's just as guilty. Besides, there's no way to prove what we do. We'll sue him for libel if he starts telling people."

Slander, Jake thought. *Libel is in print. Slander is spoken.* Didn't seem like the moment to point out the difference.

Nepto said, "He told me you have a reason for leaving town without me. But he wouldn't tell me until we got here."

"The answer," Jake said, "is probably in her suitcase."

It was a small roll-on. On the floor near the apartment door.

Ashley snapped, "You mean the one I packed because my grandmother is sick?"

"The guy whose watch you took. You threw his empty wallet into the back of my boat," Jake said. "Was it an insurance policy? Like, you could point the owner at me in case somehow this went sideways? As you kept the bundle of money that you also stole from his boat?"

Ashley said to Nepto, "I told you about the wallet. How I went back later and dropped it there. You got half the cash from it."

"One minor thing," Jake said. "The owner had an AirTag in the wallet. Next morning, he showed up to ask me why it was in the boat. Bet you didn't know about the AirTag."

Ashley grew very still.

"Look at her, Nepto," Jake said. "She knows exactly what that means."

"Ashley?" Nepto said.

She stayed silent.

Jake said, "This guy, he wants his money back."

Nepto snorted. "Hey, there was only a couple hundred bucks in his wallet."

"*Stacks* of hundreds in two bundles is what the guy told me," Jake said to Nepto. "On the houseboat. Right beside where he kept his wallet."

Jake could see Nepto slowly making the mental calculations. His face grew red.

"You held back on that?" Nepto said to Ashley. "Then packed to leave me?"

"There's nothing in the suitcase except the clothes I need for my trip," Ashley said to Nepto, the pitch of her voice rising. "You either trust him or you trust me."

"I'm not sure I could let either of you live if you really were going to rip me off and run out on me." Veins bulged in Nepto's neck. "After all the guys that I've hurt because they disrespected you. Then you do this to me?"

Nepto was a volcano ready to erupt.

Jake didn't like where this was going. Someone that big, irrational with rage, could do a lot of damage in a small place like this.

"You must both think I'm stupid." Nepto picked up a flower vase and smashed it on the floor. Ashley flinched and took a step back.

"Open the suitcase," Nepto told Jake. "Right now. Or I'll really go nuts."

His barely contained insanity seemed to fill the small apartment.

Jake took the suitcase from near the door, walked it back to the kitchen to give himself room and set it on the table. He unzipped it and lifted the lid toward Nepto. He pushed aside folded clothing until he saw a reusable grocery bag with handles. He opened the bag and saw two bundles of hundred-dollar bills inside, wrapped in clear plastic like sandwiches packed for lunch.

Ashley spoke to Jake in a tight voice. "Remember my snorkel bag? You're going to need that first pair of socks. The yellow pair."

Jake kept his eyes on Nepto as he squeezed the rolled-up pair of yellow socks. He felt a small tube inside.

"Dump the suitcase," Nepto yelled. "Flip everything onto the floor."

"Don't need to dump it," Jake said. "I found what you want to see."

He tossed both bundles onto the floor in front of Nepto, hoping it would draw him away from Ashley. Like tossing steaks over a fence to distract a Rottweiler.

But Nepto roared with rage. "I'm going to kill you both!"

He charged Jake, arms outspread. Jake tossed the socks over Nepto's head. He didn't have time to see if Ashley caught them.

Nepto didn't bother swinging at Jake. Instead he lowered his head, hoping to bear-hug Jake, flatten him on the floor and use his weight to advantage.

Jake backpedaled as he folded his arms in front of him, elbows tucked into his chest, fists held upward. That gave him space as Nepto wrapped his arms around Jake.

Jake managed to keep his balance as Nepto's momentum took them into a wall. Attempting to punch upward would have been useless. Instead Jake extended the middle knuckles of both hands and jabbed them into Nepto's throat. Just enough to distract Nepto and tilt his head back a little.

Then he slammed his forehead into Nepto's nose.

Nepto roared in pain and staggered slightly. It gave Jake just enough room to reach up and put a thumb in each side of Nepto's mouth and pull hard, hoping to shift Nepto. All Jake needed was enough room to lift a knee.

He didn't get a chance.

There was a thump.

Nepto broke his grip and lurched to the side.

Behind him Ashley had a frying pan in one hand. She must have whacked Nepto across the back of his head.

Another thump. Jake winced.

Incredibly, Nepto remained standing.

Ashley had the small tube in her other hand. Pepper spray. She aimed.

Jake dove to the side.

Chapter Thirteen

Jake grabbed Ashley and dragged her out of the apartment, slamming the door shut behind him. Crashing sounds reached them from inside.

Ashley coughed and spluttered, rubbing her eyes. "That stuff really works."

Jake felt burning pain in his throat and tears running down his face. This was just from exposure to some of the spray still hanging in the air in an enclosed space after she'd squirted it into Nepto's face. He could only imagine what it had been like for Nepto.

What Jake knew about pepper spray came from one of the combat guys who had worked with him on the Shilo base in Manitoba. The combat guy had a friend in the RCMP. As part of training at Depot Division in Regina, RCMP recruits had to let themselves get sprayed in order to learn how to fight while enduring the effects. The guy said his friend told him it was like getting hot sauce dumped onto the eyeballs and into the mouth. Instant blindness, choking sensation.

When the spray had hit Nepto full in the eyes and open mouth, he'd twisted and turned in agony, flailing those massive arms.

Smart fighters knew when to leave. So Jake had grabbed the grocery bag and the bundles of money, leaving Nepto behind to roar in anger like a crazed bull.

"I googled," Ashley said, pointing at the grocery bag. "Those stacks are high enough to be about a half million in hundreds. That's a quarter million for you. I can split my half with Nepto when he cools down."

"Trust me," Jake said. "You won't want to keep it. Not if you knew the guy who owned it. He's going to want his Rolex back too."

The crash of breaking dishes reached them.

Jake opened the door and peeked. Nepto was in the center of the kitchen, blindly sweeping his arms. Tears ran down his blotched face. The dining room table was on its side. Chairs were splintered.

"You're both dead!" Nepto roared.

Jake shut the door again. "Soon enough he's going to realize we're gone."

"Wish we could lock this from the outside," Ashley said.

"I don't think a door could stop him," Jake said. Combat skills or not, he was glad the pepper spray had been in the suitcase. Fighting Nepto had been like trying to take on the Hulk.

A door opened down the hallway. A balding, middle-age man stuck his head out. He was wearing blue pajamas. "Hey, what's going on?"

"Cops are on the way," Jake told him.

"Good. I'm trying to watch football." The man shut his door.

"You were part of this," Ashley told Jake. "Like I said to Nepto, you'll be in as much trouble as me. We're not calling the cops."

"I did a few minutes ago." Jake pulled the phone out of his pocket, increased the volume, put it on speaker and spoke into it. "Macy, you close by?"

Her voice reached them, sounding tinny. "Just parked. I'm almost at the front door."

"We're on our way out," Jake said. He ended the call and slipped the phone into his back pocket.

He looked at Ashley. "Macy is with the military police. She's been listening to the conversation from the moment I stepped into your apartment. So she knows about the half million. She's on our side, sort of," Jake continued. "Which leaves you a choice. Us—"

Another crash. More roaring.

"—or him."

Chapter Fourteen

When they reached the parking lot outside the apartment building, Macy was leaning against the hood of her Corvette, backlit by fading sunlight.

Macy pushed away from the car and extended a hand to Ashley. "Macy Templeton. Nice to meet you."

"No handcuffs?" Ashley's tone was sour.

"You've stolen money from the wrong person. And the guy upstairs threatened to kill you. I'm here to help. I think you know that." Macy turned to Jake. "Not sure I like that you went up there by yourself."

"I didn't like it either. But he was headed there to take her out of town. Seemed I needed to go along for the ride before she left with the money. I put you on the line as soon as I could."

Macy nodded. "Makes sense. I would have done the same. I heard most of what went on up there. Can't figure out what led to the yelling."

"Pepper spray," Jake said, pointing at his own stinging eyeballs. He explained what had happened.

Ashley was rubbing her eyes too.

Macy reached into the Corvette, pulled out a water bottle and handed it to Ashley. "It will help to rinse."

"I just put on mascara," Ashley said. Still, she took the bottle, poured some over her eyes and blinked.

Ashley handed the bottle to Jake. "That was okay back there. With Nepto. Thanks."

Jake handed the grocery bag to Macy, took the bottle, poured water over his eyes and blinked to try to clear them.

Macy walked to the back of the Corvette and popped the trunk. She dropped the grocery bag inside, on top of her laptop bag.

Then she closed the trunk and looked at Ashley. "Mind calling your boyfriend? Tell him to pour lukewarm water over his eyes. At least he'll be able to see. Then let him know we're waiting for him down here."

Ashley couldn't hide her astonishment. "He'll rip off our heads."

"How long do you want to be running from him?" Macy asked. "Face all the trouble he can throw at you tonight, and it will be done. Especially right now."

"Why right now?" Ashley's tone shifted to defiance mode.

"Because you have the military backing you up."

Macy's quiet confidence seemed to work.

Ashley made the call and hung up. "He'll be down. No surprise. He promised to tear us apart."

"Do you blame him?" Macy asked. "I doubt it's the money he cared about."

Macy slipped around to the other side of the Corvette. She slid inside and turned on her stereo. Classical music. It was a good stereo system, and it sounded especially good with the sunroof open.

She came back to Ashley and Jake. "When he gets here, I'd like both of you leaning against the car. Make it casual. I don't want it to seem like it's three against one."

"I'll be ready to run," Ashley said. "Trust me on that."

"You won't have to run. Jake and I are going to play good cop, good cop."

Jake tilted his head, puzzled.

"Easiest way is if we get him on our side," Macy told Jake. "Follow my lead, follow your instincts."

Ashley leaned against the back fender of the Corvette. Jake took a position at the front fender, almost where Macy had been waiting for them earlier. The music in the background relaxed him, and he realized that Macy had chosen the music for that reason.

It didn't take long for Nepto to step out of the building. Even this far into the evening, there was enough sunlight to see that his face was blotched from the pepper spray. His nose was running, his eyes angry and red. He looked very uncomfortable.

He marched toward them, his fingers curled into fists. A few steps away he stopped.

"Seriously?" he said. "What kind of crap music is that?"

"Claude Debussy," Macy said. "Titled 'Clair de lune.' It's a musical description of moonlight. Like it?"

"Do I look like the type of person who does?"

"By your muscle structure, you look like the type of person capable of dedication and hard work. As a military person, I'm impressed with your discipline. Jake?"

"He's impressive," Jake said.

Nepto seemed to relax. Just a little.

"You know Jake already," Macy said. "Mind if I introduce myself?"

"What I mind is getting backstabbbed and pepper-sprayed," Nepto said, scowling. "Backstabbed more than the pepper spray. I'm going to—"

Macy stepped forward, hand extended. "Macy Templeton. Thanks for coming down to talk. I always appreciate someone who comes into a conversation with an open mind."

Nepto ignored her hand. "Why should I care who you are?"

Despite his words, Jake saw that Nepto had uncurled his fingers. His shoulders seemed less tight. Jake began to understand why Macy was playing it this way.

"Macy's been helping me," Jake said. "You open to giving her a chance to do the same for you?"

Macy's voice remained friendly as she spoke above the background of the classical music. "In my working hours, I'm an investigator for the armed forces."

"What?"

She reached into her back pocket, pulled out her ID and handed it to Nepto. "Here's my identification."

He spoke as he read it, eyes watering. "Canadian Forces Military Police."

"I'm off duty tonight. I just want to pass along some helpful information for you. Remember Alfie McTaggert? Rented a houseboat from you the other day."

Nepto nodded.

"I was able to run his name. McTaggert owns pawn shops in Edmonton and Calgary, and a vending-machine company that services all of Western Canada. Convenient for him because of all the cash involved. Lots of rumors about criminal connections to bike gangs, which Jake can confirm from this morning. People who cross him get hurt. The cops know all about it, but nothing sticks. Witnesses tend to change their minds before getting to court."

"Bike gangs." Nepto shifted from foot to foot.

"He brought in some bikers from Kamloops to mess with me," Jake said. "A guy like you would have been helpful to have around."

Jake wondered if he was pushing it too hard, trying to get Nepto on their side. But Nepto actually gave Jake a curt nod of acknowledgment.

"Something was taken from McTaggert last night on a houseboat he rented from you," Macy said. "Since he didn't report it to police, that means he'd prefer to take matters into his own hands. If he gets it back, though, it's like nothing happened. Police won't have to look into any of this."

"Any of this?"

"Remember, we're having an open conversation, and I'm off duty. In theory, if things have disappeared in the past from houseboats, there's nothing the police can do about it. If it continues, that's a different matter. You look like a decent person. I'd hate to have to come back with some RCMP friends for an official conversation. Understand?"

Nepto nodded again.

Good cop, good cop. Jake was amazed at how much Nepto's temper had cooled. He glanced back at Ashley, noting her crossed arms.

"Tonight is your chance to choose a future that won't involve police for any reason," Macy continued. "Whatever has happened between you and Ashley proves that relationships can be complicated and don't always work out the way you want. The important thing is you move on and don't make the situation worse."

"That money," Nepto said. "It's going back to the guy? Not to Ashley?"

"It's not her money." Macy extended her hand again. "I also suggest that you avoid any less-than-civil conversations in the future with Jake or Ashley. Please let me know we are good here."

Nepto looked away for a few moments. When he turned his head toward Macy again, he accepted her handshake. "This sucks. But yeah, we're good."

He looked at Ashley one more time. He opened his mouth to say something to her, then closed his mouth again and shook his head.

Jake couldn't read Nepto's expression. Sadness? Regret?

Nepto walked toward his black pickup truck, the music from Macy's car playing as softly as the last of the sunlight played on his broad back and shoulders. He climbed into the truck, shut the door with a quiet click, started the engine and drove away without a backward glance.

Jake realized that what he'd just learned about dealing with angry opponents was far more impressive than anything any combat soldier had taught him.

Chapter Fifteen

Jake sat on his uncle's dock with Macy in a chair beside him. Another day with clear skies. Each of them nursed mugs with coffee.

Macy looked relaxed. Jake was not.

He checked his watch. Nine o'clock in the morning.

Alfie McTaggert had already responded to his text and given Jake his location on the Maps app on Jake's phone. It would take at least 45 minutes to get there. If Ashley didn't show up in the next ten minutes, he would be taking his uncle's ski boat onto the lake by himself.

"How was the conversation with your mom this morning?" Macy asked. "Not that it's my business."

"You checked her files, I'm guessing."

"I did."

"So you know."

"That she's struggling with an adjustment to civilian life."

"Yeah. I hate that I'm making it even tougher for her. I can't change the way I feel, and it adds to her stress."

Jake had not expected to admit how he felt to anyone. But something about the way Macy listened made it easy to talk to her.

"Jake, don't beat yourself up. People can't choose how they feel. They can only control their actions."

"I should lie to my mother? Tell her I'm okay with the price that our family has paid for military service? No problem I didn't grow up with a dad? No problem I spent half my life without her in it while she was gone on tours, leaving me behind with neighbors? Switch bases every few years, put me in new schools?"

"Being open about it would help. She'd have a chance to explain her choices. Hey, I don't have kids, and it's still tough enough in the military. I can't imagine it for a single mom, the sacrifices and the conflict between duty and family. It would make a difference if you at least acknowledged to your mom that you know it's been tough."

"For what, though?" Jake had held onto his bitterness far too long. It felt good to let it spill. "Special recognition on Remembrance Day? The rest of the year, nobody in this country cares about the military. Civilians have no idea what the armed forces do for them. No idea at all. Not what the soldiers face. Not what the families face.

Difference is, kids of soldiers didn't sign up for what they have to deal with."

"I hear you. It's like Mother's Day, right?"

"Mother's Day?" Jake echoed.

"Sure. That's the day a mom gets a bit of recognition, but the rest of the year, day in and day out, moms bear the burden of making sure the family is doing okay. I don't think they do it for thanks or recognition. Your mom ever ask you for thanks? You let her know year-round how special she is to you? Or do you save it for one day? Like the country does for Remembrance Day?"

Jake had no reply.

"And you're right," she continued. "Military kids don't sign up for it. But kids never get a choice of what families they are born into. That's how life works. Some kids get good parents, some kids get horrible parents. Some are born into money. Some are not. Ashley, for example. You never know what brought her to how she is today. Your only choice is the attitude you are going take into what life gives you."

Again Jake opted for silence.

"Yeah, that was preachy, but get over it," Macy said, as if she understood he needed time to think. "I'm going to grab some coffee. Back soon."

Before she could get up from the chair, though, Ashley came around the corner of the back of the house. She stepped onto the dock. Ball cap, sunglasses, long-sleeved T-shirt, jeans.

Jake and Macy stood.

Halfway across the lake, a ski boat passed, with a family enjoying the wind in their faces.

Ashley reached them, crossed her arms and said, "Not too late to change your minds. Nepto's out, so that means we could do a three-way split. Hundred sixty-six grand each. Or how about 175 to each of you, and I'll settle for 150."

Macy laughed. "Don't blame you for trying. Just like I hope you don't blame me for asking if you brought the Daytona."

"I told you last night. Nepto has it."

"You did tell me that last night. That he's walking away with something he can sell for a minimum fifty grand, and you're ending up with nothing."

"Totally nothing. That's why I insisted on going with Jake. To make sure you two don't keep the money. If I can't have it, neither can you."

"Are you sure this is about the money?" Macy asked.

"You're kidding, right? Why wouldn't it be about the money?"

"Jake thinks he has a good idea of how it worked. Jake?"

"Jake already did his detective thing last night," Ashley said. "Yeah, congratulations. Nepto would keep his eye open for renters with expensive watches.

I'd do the cat-burglar thing at night while they were asleep on the houseboat."

"Jake?"

"It has to be a certain type of rental party," Jake said. "Mainly all guys. Who pack in lots of booze. Drunks don't wake up easily. If they do, they are probably going to be happy to see a babe in a bikini at three in the morning who tells them a story about an assassin game and getting onto the wrong boat. With that photo of Nepto on your phone to prove the story is true. You can party with them if they want and then escape. Or, worst-case scenario, you've got pepper spray for backup and a dive into the lake so Nepto can pick you up and make a getaway."

"Why does this feel like a television-show wrap-up?" Ashley said.

"There's a point to this," Macy said. "Jake, would you mind continuing?"

"Drunk guys wake up to a missing watch, they convince themselves they lost it in the night, maybe dropped it into the lake. And they can file insurance claims. So you only do this once in a while. When there's a watch worth stealing and the risk is minimal."

"The point here?" Ashley said, faking a yawn.

"You're the brains behind this," Macy said. "That's the first point. You are extremely intelligent and street-smart. The job you have probably isn't much of a challenge for you."

Jake couldn't read what Ashley was thinking. The sunglasses on her face were huge, and the lid of her ball cap pushed down. He guessed she didn't want Alfie McTaggert to get a good look at her face.

"What I do is about 95 percent routine and boredom," Macy continued. "Then there's about 5 percent that feels like the best part of a television show. Going into a takedown, not sure which way it will end. Or that moment when everything adds up, and you know who did it. I think it's the same for you. It's not about the money, it's about the thrill. Slipping into a dark houseboat at three in the morning, playing a game with high stakes and coming out the winner."

Ashley stepped past Macy and down into the ski boat. She looked up and said, "How about we get this over with and return the money?"

Macy didn't lose any friendliness. "You bet. One thing I didn't mention. Thanks to Jake, you'll both be under drone surveillance the entire time."

Chapter Sixteen

They cruised through the Sicamous Narrows at a slow speed that left no wake. Jake stood behind the wheel, Ashley sat on the passenger side of the front seat. Both were wearing life jackets.

Alfie McTaggert had insisted that Jake use the sharing feature of the Find My app so that McTaggert could track the location of *Shock Wave*. Ironic, Jake thought. Macy had insisted on the same thing.

It looked like they would be on time. Right after the drop-off, Jake would be turning off the feature.

No way did he want McTaggert tracking him ever again.

"Seriously?" Ashley said. Her first words since leaving the dock. "You asked for a drone?"

"I can't watch you every second while I'm at the wheel," Jake said. "Easy enough for you to knock me out, take the boat to a different marina and walk away with the cash. As you've pointed out, it's almost a half million dollars. Nothing so far suggests she has any reason to trust you with that kind of money. It was either a drone or handcuffs. But handcuffing you wouldn't be smart. You might drown if there was a boat accident."

"I'm touched by your concern." They were leaving the narrows. Ashley craned her head to look upward.

As she did, the boat hit a wave that threw her off-balance. She fell into Jake and grabbed his shoulders. For a moment their faces were only inches apart as she gripped him. In that moment, unsteady, she seemed vulnerable instead of tough. Jake wondered what it would be like to kiss her. Then she pushed away, as if regretting how she had let the moment linger, their faces that close.

"It's a bluff," Ashley said. She glanced upward again. "There's no drone up there."

Jake took a deep breath. *Fine.* He could be as tough as she was. "When I asked Macy about surveillance, she called in a favor to get a military drone. From the air force. The operator is still on the base, controlling it on a laptop via satellite. It's about 25,000 feet up. Camera is good enough to read the year on a dime if I held it out on my hand."

"Good thing you didn't try to kiss me," Ashley said. "That would have been awkward. Your military buddies watching and all."

Heat rushed into Jake's face. "Kiss you? That's the last—"

"How does she have that kind of pull?" Ashley interrupted, smirking.

And how did she manage to keep him so unnerved? Jake was glad for a chance to focus on answering her question. "Macy conveniently forgot to mention her rank to us. She's a colonel, one step short of the top rank, general."

"You know this how?"

"I asked around."

"She knows you know?"

"Why spoil her fun?"

Clear of the Sicamous Narrows, they passed a crowded beach, then entered Shuswap Lake. Jake glanced at his phone. GPS showed him he was on a straight line to the houseboat.

Jake added speed, and the breeze pulled at his hair. The electric outboards were quiet, so he didn't need to raise his voice much to speak to Ashley.

"Two nights ago on his houseboat," Jake said. "When you found him asleep, he wasn't wearing the Daytona, was he?"

"You like this, playing detective?"

"He told me he wears a Fitbit to monitor his sleep. You had that little flashlight, started looking around. Found the watch and wallet and the bundles of money in the same place."

"What does it matter?" she asked.

"You had a pouch in your snorkel bag. You loaded the watch and the wallet and the money into that pouch. Hung the pouch from the ladder on my uncle's ski boat before you climbed back into the boat so I wouldn't find anything in case I looked. I assume you came back for the pouch later, while I was asleep."

"Good work, detective," she said. "Your turn to answer something. Your tone of voice, talking about what I did—does it make you feel superior to be judging me?"

"Where I grew up," Jake said, "people didn't take from other people, they made sacrifices for other people."

Jake thought about a story his mother had told him.

"My mom's a medic," Jake said. "One time she was wrapping a chest wound on a soldier that she knew wouldn't make it. She pulled out the soldier's cell phone. She had to wipe away the soldier's blood on the phone to be able to activate the screen. She unlocked it with facial recognition, which wouldn't work until she wiped blood off the soldier's face. She found the contact that said *Mom*. Hit the button so he could talk to her, giving the mom one last chance to talk to her son who was dying halfway across the world. My mom, she's dealing with dozens of memories like that. Sacrifices she's made. Sacrifices people around her make. All the time."

In that moment Jake had a major realization. He was proud of his mom, proud that she had made those sacrifices.

"Reason I'm not going to tell you any of my stories," Ashley said, "is I don't want your sympathy.

Yeah, hanging out with Nepto, not the smartest. It's why I was doing my best to escape. But compared to where I came from, he wasn't the worst alternative. At least he tried to protect me. You're lucky. People around you make sacrifices for other people. People around me made me wish I'd never been born."

She got up from the passenger seat and moved to the back of the boat, leaving Jake with thoughts about his mom. And about Ashley. And how he'd misjudged them both.

Chapter Seventeen

Alfie McTaggert had chosen a spot almost in the center of the lake. He was standing on the back deck of the houseboat as they approached. Alone. In shorts, no shirt. Not much chance of sunburn, Jake thought. The guy was too hairy.

Jake eased back on the throttle and then reversed, bringing the boat to a standstill with maybe ten paces of water between them. The deck of the houseboat had a small table ringed by deck chairs. Something about half the size of a toaster sat on the side of the table.

"You'll notice I dropped all my party people off at a local marina." Gone was the fake friendliness from the morning before. "We don't need any witnesses for this. I can't say I'm happy you brought some broad."

That irritated Jake, the term *broad*.

"Wait," McTaggert said. "She's the one who was with you that night. The one in the video."

"Your money is here in this gym bag," Jake said. He held it up for McTaggert to see. He clipped the handles of the gym bag to a life jacket. "I'm going to throw it in your direction. You'll be able to snag it with the lifeguard rescue pole hanging by the ladder."

"Hey, you, broad," McTaggert said. "Take off the hat and sunglasses. I want to see your face."

"Not for someone who calls me a broad," Ashley said.

"You don't get to find out who she is," Jake said. "This is just between you and me."

McTaggert shook his head. "Yes I do. You remember my friends on your dock? One phone call, and they're headed this way from Kamloops."

"Send them," Jake said. "I'm not returning the money because I'm afraid of you. I'm returning it because it's yours."

"What about the watch?"

Jake reached into his back pocket and pulled out a watch. Stainless steel band. Large face. He dangled it so that McTaggert had a good look. Then dropped it back in the bag.

"You don't leave until I've counted all the money," McTaggert said. He pointed at a small toaster-shaped object on the table behind him. "See that? It's a bill counter. Otherwise it would take forever."

"Fine by me," Jake said. "You ready with the rescue pole?"

"You could simply tie up to the houseboat."

"Nope," Jake said. "You've made it clear that you are a dangerous man. I'll throw it somewhere between us."

As McTaggert turned his back toward the ladder that led to the roof of the houseboat, Jake slipped the watch out of the gym bag and hid it in his palm. He left the gym bag slightly unzipped. Not enough for money to fly out when he tossed it.

McTaggert grabbed the pole, which had a standard pool-safety hook attached to it. He moved back to the edge of the houseboat.

"Toss it," McTaggert said. "I'm ready."

Jake threw the life jacket with the gym bag clipped in place. He released the watch from his hand at the same time. It flew in a high arc and splashed into the lake, just short of the houseboat. A moment later the life jacket slapped onto the surface and bobbed.

"My watch!" McTaggert screamed. "It's four hundred feet deep here. Can't wait to get a video of my biker friends breaking your arm. Maybe I *will* send them after your mom too."

Time and again, the combat specialists had warned Jake that emotional reactions were dangerous.

Usually he listened.

Not this time. He dove into the water to cover the distance to the houseboat.

Chapter Eighteen

Seconds later he was at the ladder to the houseboat. Yeah, Ashley might leave him stranded. But there was the drone. She knew about it. And even if she decided it didn't matter, Jake didn't care.

He was ice-cold angry.

He pulled himself up the ladder, his clothes dripping with water.

"Have you lost your mind?" Ashley yelled from *Shock Wave*. Jake ignored her.

McTaggert was waiting for him, holding the rescue pole sideways, ready to swing.

"I'm tired of your threats," Jake said. Moving closer on the rear deck.

"You owe me a Daytona," McTaggert answered.

"We'll get my uncle's insurance to deal with it. Let's call the RCMP, file a report. Get them out here right now."

"Like that's going to happen," McTaggert said. "I'll be sending my friends on bikes in your direction."

He jabbed the pole in Ashley's direction. "Her too." He raised his voice to Ashley. "You are nothing more than trailer trash. My biker friends are going to love you."

"Two things," Jake said through clenched teeth. "Let's get the first out of the way. I want to be clear. You confirm you don't want to call the cops for an insurance report?"

"I don't do insurance," McTaggert said. "Good luck with the bikers. Second thing?"

"An apology. To my friend."

McTaggert responded by swinging the pole sideways at Jake's head in a violent slice, aiming the hook at Jake's neck.

Instead of trying to dodge or duck it, Jake chose an unexpected reaction. He had already made the simple calculation of leverage. The outer end of the pole had the most speed. The inner end, in McTaggert's hand, far less. The outer end would move ten feet, the inner end only a foot.

Jack leapt forward and twisted sideways to block the pole with open hands. As he landed, the pole slapped into his palms, a sensation that burned like it was a branding iron.

Jake grunted, wrenched the pole loose from McTaggert and smashed it down on the deck railing. It snapped in two, leaving Jake with a jagged rod about three feet long. A nice weapon.

McTaggert stared at him. Stunned.

So many options for Jake now. The man was

slow and out of shape. What Jake wanted to do was beat him as if he were a piñata.

Instead Jake patted McTaggert's cheek, proving he could have just as easily broken the man's nose. Jake transferred his cold rage into a quiet voice, barely above a whisper.

"It's just you and me, no biker friends." Jake patted McTaggert's other cheek, showing he was in total control. "Count the money. While you're doing that, think through exactly how you're going to apologize to her when you're finished."

McTaggert blinked a few times. He seemed to read correctly how difficult it was for Jake to hold back.

McTaggert lifted the gym bag. He backed away to the small table, keeping his eyes on Jake. He unwrapped the bundles of money and stacked the bills into the machine. Its whirring was easy to hear.

How many one-hundred-dollar bills? He did the math. Five thousand. Five thousand!

It took nearly five minutes to count, the houseboat rocking on the water.

"All there?" Jake said.

McTaggert nodded. Watchful. Jake knew he was afraid.

"Remember the reason you threatened to torch my uncle's property?" Jake said. "You told me my mom and I had nothing to lose. But a guy who can let a Rolex drop into a lake and not bother with insurance? That's someone with a lot to lose."

Jake tapped him lightly with the broken pole.

"Now. I know who you are," Jake said. "I'm going to make you a promise, *Alfie McTaggert*. Anything happens to my uncle or mother, I will hunt you down. If you send bikers after me, they better kill me, because that's the only thing that's going to stop me. And if they do kill me, I also have powerful friends. Military. Trained to hunt and destroy. Whether it's me or my friends, you'll never know what hit you."

Jake paused to let the shock wave of the threat wash over McTaggert. "Nod if you understand."

McTaggert waited ten seconds. Then nodded.

"That takes us to the second thing," Jake said. He pointed at Ashley, who was watching intently across the gap between boats. "My friend gets your apology. Or all that money goes into the lake."

Chapter Nineteen

"I can fight my own battles," Ashley told Jake. "I've been doing it my entire life."

There had been five minutes of silence between the two of them, five minutes since Jake had made it back into the boat and turned it toward Sicamous, the houseboat now well behind them. Five minutes waiting for his heart rate to slow down.

"Your own battles?"

"Making some hood apologize to me for an insult. Like I'm this helpless damsel in need of a white knight."

"Here's what my mom taught me," Jake said. "You can use strength to push people around, or you can use strength to help them. Has nothing to do with damsels and knights. I was in a position of strength. Could just as easily have been you helping me instead. You know, like when you whacked Nepto on the head with a frying pan."

She gave it couple of seconds of thought. "Fair enough."

The breeze felt good to Jake. His clothes were nearly dry already in the heat.

"Whose watch was it?" Ashley asked.

"Macy and I drove to Kamloops last night to a Walmart to find a cheap one that looked the same."

"Your idea or Macy's?"

"Mine," Jake said. "After Macy mentioned that when you and Nepto stole watches, the owners would report it to insurance companies."

"That's why I never felt bad. Insurance companies have lots of money," Ashley said.

"Paid by people like my mom," Jake said, without thinking how it might sound to Ashley. "Who don't have lots of money."

She glared. "How about stop judging? Let's just say I really know all the ins and outs of social-service agencies. And what it's like to go hungry. It was either look out for myself or let others destroy me."

She moved to the back of the boat. Jake thought about what Macy had said. People don't get to choose what they are born into. He didn't have the right to judge Ashley.

"Hey," he said. "I'm sorry."

"Not as sorry as I am," she answered.

Just like on the ride to the houseboat, Ashley didn't say a word the entire way back. Or on the dock when she walked away.

Chapter Twenty

Jake and Macy sat opposite each other at a booth by the window. The Corvette was in the same place, Macy's laptop, lid closed, on the table.

It was noon, and she'd ordered the same breakfast. Their plates had been cleared, and both had coffees in front of them.

A black pickup truck turned into the parking lot.

"Nepto," Jake said, tensing.

He watched as Nepto stopped the truck. Ashley stepped down from the passenger side. She waved and shut the door. Nepto drove away. Ashley walked into the restaurant. Macy waved her over.

As Ashley neared the booth, Macy said, "Jake, mind moving over to make room?"

Ashley slid into the booth. "Hey, thanks for texting back. I just wanted to drop something off."

"Not my business," Macy said, "but you and Nepto?"

"We're not back together. More of a closure thing. Both of us agreed it was time to move on from what wasn't good."

Jake felt his abdomen muscles relax.

"You okay?" Macy asked Ashley.

"Sad. But I think that's the way it should be. When I chose money over him, it told me enough. Not sure I liked what I learned. About the relationship. And me."

Ashley opened her hand and placed a watch on the table. It had a white face with dials in the center and a gold ring on the outside. The band was stainless steel.

"Other reason for meeting Nepto," Ashley said. "I talked him into giving back the Daytona."

Macy looked her straight in the eyes, and Jake easily read her expression. Skeptical and letting it show.

"You *are* good," Ashley said to Macy. "Here's the truth. Nepto never had it. I just want to make some changes, feel better about myself. Do with the Daytona what you want."

Macy said, "I appreciate this. And your honesty. We'll get the watch back to McTaggert. He might want to sell it to help cover his upcoming legal fees."

"Legal fees?" Ashley echoed.

"If you hang around, it will make more sense. Jake and I are waiting for a text. In the meantime, there's something I want to run past you. Want to order breakfast?"

Ashley said, "I could use a coffee. Who would eat breakfast this late in the day?"

"Are you kidding?" Macy said. "Breakfast at any time—"

Macy's cell phone dinged. She glanced at her text. She opened her laptop and said, "Ashley, remember that drone I told you about? You're both going to want to see this."

Macy spun the laptop to face them and squeezed in on their side of the booth so that all three of them could watch. "I'm hooked up to what the operator is viewing."

The image was as clear as if they were sitting in a chair directly above the houseboat. It showed the small table on the back deck, the money counter still in place and stacks of bills beside it. A small boat was tied to the houseboat.

Alfie McTaggert stood on one side of the table, a dark-haired man on the other. The aerial view showed that he was balding on top.

There was a cardboard tube at the man's feet. The man was holding what looked like an unrolled poster. The image was so crisp that Jake could tell it wasn't a poster but an oil painting with weird abstract figures.

Jake said, "If you screenshot that, a Google images search could tell us what it is, right?"

Before Macy could answer, her cell phone rang. She listened for a few moments, then hung up and spoke to Jake. "That's exactly what our RCMP friends were doing. Shouldn't be long now until this gets even more fun."

Chapter Twenty-One

Macy moved back to the other side of the booth and spoke to Jake. "Mind telling Ashley what you remembered from McTaggert's first conversation with you?"

"So I can feel like a kid in class brought up to the blackboard?"

Macy laughed. "Point taken." She took a sip of coffee, then said to Ashley, "McTaggert wondered if someone had sent Jake from Vancouver to get the money. That suggested to Jake that a deal was in place. Which, as Jake also suggested, makes sense. McTaggert lives in Alberta. Sicamous is a good midway point to meet someone from Vancouver. Out on the lake in a houseboat would make it totally private. Plus McTaggert set a specific deadline to get the money back. Jake made the argument to me that it was unlikely the deal was legit. Suggested a plan to watch with a drone. And get a search warrant in place. Jake's argument was solid."

"Search warrant for a drone?" Ashley said.

"Part of police work is making sure that every-thing holds up in court." Macy tapped the computer screen. "The RCMP is not going to make the bust until our Vancouver guy is in his boat and moving away with the money. Any guess why?"

Ashley gave it some thought. "Because a drone can read the numbers on a dime from 25,000 feet, Jake made sure to hold the bundles so it would be easy to record the numbers on the top bills. They want to catch the guy with those bills. Bet it helped that they could get video of him counting the money while we waited."

"I like the way you think," Macy said. "That, along with footage of him taking money onto the boat, should do it. Along with, if needed, assault charges. We've got some clear footage of him attacking Jake with that pole. Good thing the drone is sharp enough to pick up that all Jake did in return was pat his face."

Another text came in. Macy read it out loud. "*Google results show that it's a Picasso. Stolen from a private art collection six months ago.*"

She grinned at Jake. "Good job."

Ashley said to Macy, "This is one of your cases with a bit of a thrill, right? The 5 percenters?"

Macy smiled. "The same kind of thrill that put you onto houseboats at three in the morning. Which brings me to what I wanted to talk about. How interested are you in this? You know, in case you were open to considering time in the armed forces.

I have a specific job in mind, but you'd have to sign up first. Spend time as a private on a naval training base."

"Navy?" Ashley said. "As in, travel to different places?"

"No special treatment. You sign up, it's a three-year commitment. If you like the life, you can sign up for another tour. Then who knows where in the world you'd go."

"Navy," Ashley said. "I've never been outside the province. It might be a good time for a new start."

Macy looked at Jake. "Actually, I could use two sets of eyes. Both of you are smart. You'd make a good team. Telling your mom that you're okay with all her years in the military is one thing. But signing up yourself—"

Macy's cell phone dinged again. "Here it is. They're about to move in."

She slid back in on their side of the booth to watch. The view on the computer screen was now at a wider angle, showing four boats in the center of the lake. The houseboat was stationary. A second boat was speeding toward it, leaving an obvious wake. An RCMP boat. Another RCMP boat was closing in on the fourth, which was moving away from the houseboat, with the money from the deal.

Bingo.

Jake remembered what Ashley had said to him earlier, as they'd been cruising through the Sicamous Narrows to return the money to McTaggert.

You like this, playing detective.

He liked the thought.

He imagined more time around Ashley. He was surprised to realize he liked that thought too.

He also imagined his next call to his mom. To tell her he understood a little better. No, a lot better. He was proud of the military. He knew it would help take away guilt from the conflict she carried as a single mother torn between her duty and what it did to her kid.

"Just so you know," Jake told Macy, "I don't need a new start."

"Sorry to hear that," Macy said.

"But I'd still like to hear more about your offer"—he paused for a single beat—"Colonel."

The lift of surprise in Macy's eyebrows was a satisfying reward. So was the smile on Ashley's face.

Acknowledgments

Much gratitude to MCpl (Ret'd) Natalie Forcier, CD for helping make sure the military aspects of the story are accurate, and even more gratitude for your insightful discussions on life in the Canadian Armed Forces.

And many many thanks to Shelley Davis Forman, the wonderful principal at Arrowwood Community School, and my friends there who were part of the story-writing process and made so many valuable suggestions as a team of amazing editors:

Chloe Kuntz

Jamie Liu

Nelly Loepky

Ayana Spotted Eagle

Hudson Big Snake

Conan Broad Scalplock

Sonnie Melting Tallow

Makinley Wells

Mica Bernardo

Mateo Diaz

Gage Kuntz

Kyzin Marshman

David Rempel

Kayleb Scalplock Fox

Sigmund Brouwer is the award-winning author of over 100 books for young readers, with over five million books in print. He has won a Christy Book of the Year and an Arthur Ellis Award, and some of his titles were finalists for the TD Canadian Children's Literature Award (twice) and the Red Maple Award. Sigmund has captivated students with his Story Ninja writing program during his school visits, reaching over one million students since 1990. His many books in the Orca Sports, Orca Soundings and Orca Currents lines have changed the lives of countless striving readers. Sigmund lives in Red Deer, Alberta.